Supermom

Written by Mick Manning and illustrated by Brita Granström

Albert Whitman & Company
Morton Grove, Illinois

Supermom is everywhere!
Swinging, swooping, swimming, scooting.

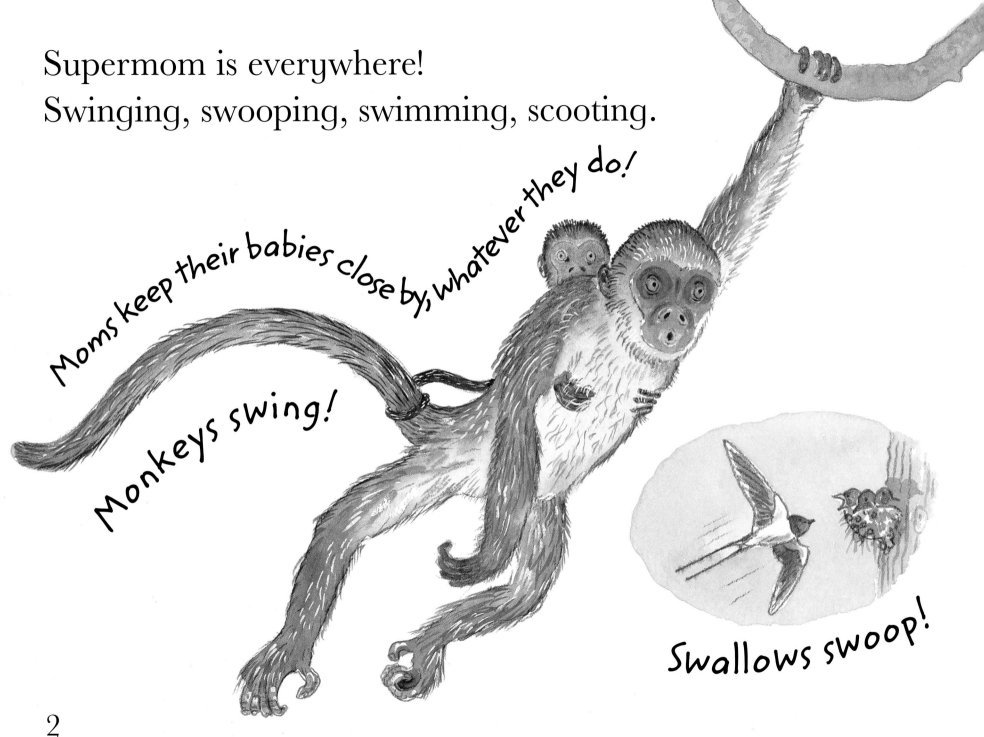

Moms keep their babies close by, whatever they do!

Monkeys swing!

Swallows swoop!

Supermom comes in all shapes
and sizes, with lots of legs,
lots of fur, a tail, or even scales!

Mouthbreeders shelter their
babies in their mouths!

We call the person who gave birth to us "mom." We can call the grownup who takes care of us "mom," too.

Wildebeest moms have horns.

Even bugs can be good moms!

5

Supermom has babies!
She lays eggs—or she carries
her babies inside her body
until they're born.

Some snake moms guard their eggs.

We all need a mom or we couldn't be born.
Moms bring new life into the world.

Blue whales are the biggest moms on earth!

6

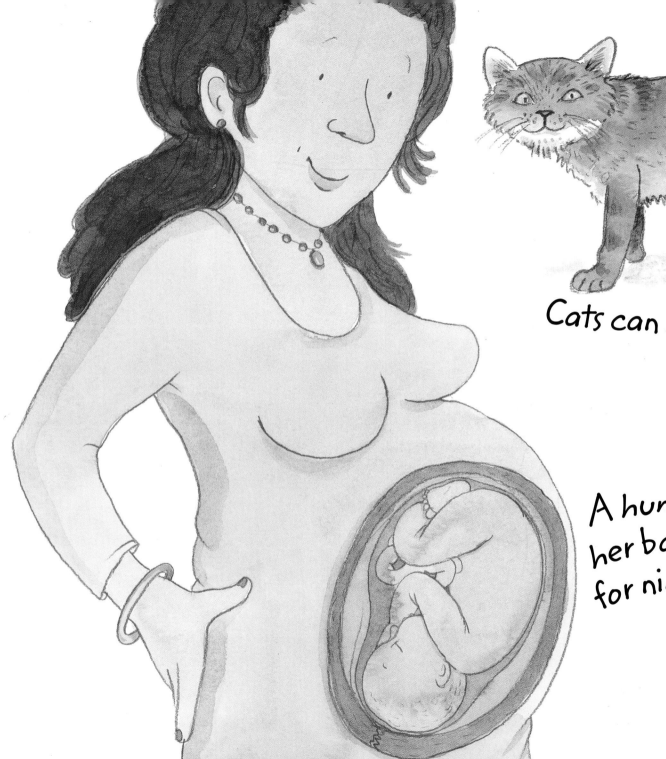

Cats can have lots of babies.

A human mom carries her baby inside her body for nine months.

7

Supermom knows the best games—
hide and seek, tickle, horsey,
and lots of others.

Weasel moms have all
kinds of tricks!

Just like you, wolf cubs learn by
playing with their moms.

Supermom talks to her babies—
in lots of different ways!

11

Supermom will do anything for her little ones!
She'll go out in a storm to get food.

Penguins travel for days to find fish for their babies.
Your mom goes out in all kinds of weather for your food, too!

Supermom is brave! If you threaten her babies, she'll scratch! She'll fight! She'll bark! She'll bite!

From swan moms to insect moms, many animal moms will fight to protect their babies.

15

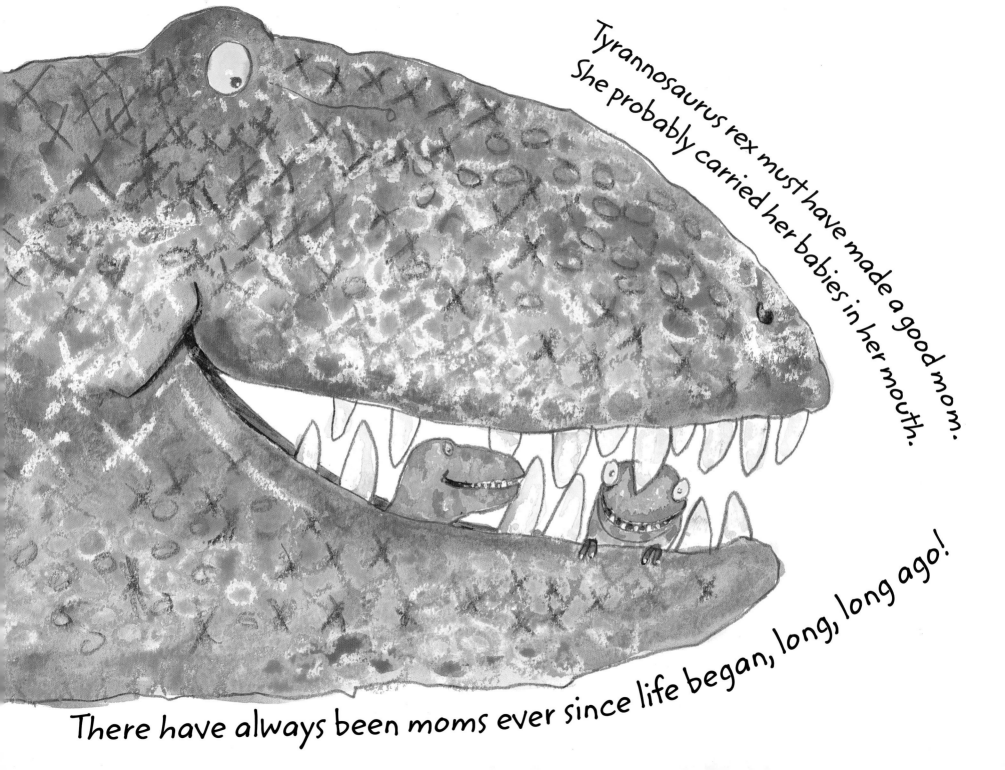

Tyrannosaurus rex must have made a good mom. She probably carried her babies in her mouth.

There have always been moms ever since life began, long, long, long ago!

Supermom is gentle!
She might look scary, but she always
treats her babies **very** carefully.

Moms are very gentle
with their children.

Supermom knows best!
She knows just what her baby likes to eat.
Worms, beetles, or bananas?
Supermom even knows your favorites.

Different baby animals like different baby foods— and moms know best!

Wasp grubs eat caterpillars. Osprey chicks eat fish... What do you like best?

19

Supermom makes sure bath time is the best time! She keeps her babies nice and clean.

Babies need to be clean to grow up healthy.

20

Supermom is a nest-builder, a burrower,
a cave-dweller—a homemaker.
She tucks in her babies in all sorts of cozy places!

A chimney!

A bird's nest!

A hole in the ground!

Even a crack
in a wall . . .

or a little wooden bed!

24

Supermom is a cuddle expert!
She'll nurse her babies to sleep, holding them
close while they have the happiest dreams.

Cuddling is a good way for mom and baby to show how much they love each other.

Supermom is wide awake!
Even on the darkest night, she's always
ready to feed her hungry babies.

Owl moms hunt mice in the dark.

Human babies can wake up anytime to feed!

27

There have always been different kinds of supermoms…

and there always will be.

Quack!

Eek!

All

Cheep!

28

Squeak!

Oink!

Sssss!

moms are supermoms!

Grrr!

Prrr!

Supermom Index

Ant – See page 23. An ant's nest is started by a queen ant. She lays all the eggs that hatch into the thousands of ants that will live there.

Barn owl – See page 26. Barn owl moms hunt for rats and mice to feed to their babies.

Blue whale – See page 6. Blue whale moms have a baby every two or three years.

Brown bear – See page 5. Brown bear moms look after their cubs for over three years.

Cat – See page 7. Cat moms can have a litter of kittens once a year.

Dolphin – See pages 10 and 11. Dolphin moms look after their babies for about a year and a half.

Lynx – See page 25. Lynx moms have between one and five kittens at a time.

Monkey – See page 2. Monkeys carry their babies on their backs or around their tummies.

Mouse – See page 22. Mouse moms can nest under floorboards or even in old birds' nests.

Mouthbreeder – See page 4. A type of fish that protect their babies inside their mouths.

Orca – See page 3. Orcas are sometimes called killer whales. Orca moms teach their babies to hunt.

Ostrich – See pages 10 and 11. Ostrich moms lay about fifteen eggs at a time.

Penguin – See page 12. Emperor penguin moms bring food for their chicks back from the sea.

Polar bear – See pages 10 and 11. Polar bears usually have two cubs at a time.

Rabbit – See page 22. Rabbit moms have lots of babies—up to eighty-four every year!

Raccoon – See page 22. Raccoon moms often bring up their babies in towns and cities.

Snake – See page 6. Not all snake moms guard their eggs. Some just lay them and leave them.

Swallow – See page 2. Swallow moms feed their babies mushed-up insects.

Swan – See page 14. Mute swans will attack if you go near their nests.

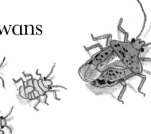

Tiger – See page 20. Tiger moms take care of their cubs for two to three years.

Tyrannosaurus rex – See page 16. *Tyrannosaurus rex* was the largest meat-eating mom that ever existed.

Wasp – See page 19. A digger wasp digs a small tunnel and lays her egg there.

Weasel – See page 8. Weasel moms are fierce if their babies are in danger.

Wild boar – See pages 10 and 11. Boar moms have up to ten babies at a time.

Wildebeest – See page 5. A wildebeest mom has one baby a year. She always keeps an eye out for danger from lions or hyenas.

Wolf – See page 8. Wolf moms have about seven cubs at one time.

For our mums—and mums everywhere.

—M.M. and B.G.

What about superdad?

First published in 1999 by Franklin Watts,
96 Leonard Street, London EC2A 4XD.

Library of Congress Cataloging-in-Publication Data

Manning, Mick.
    Supermom / by Mick Manning ; illustrated by Brita Granström.
    p. cm.
    ISBN 0-8075-7666-2 (hardcover)
1. Parental behavior in animals–Juvenile literature.
2. Mothers–Juvenile literature. [1. Mothers. 2. Animals–Habits and
behavior. 3. Parental behavior in animals.] I. Granström, Brita, ill.
II. Title.
    QL762 .M33 2001
    591.56'3—dc21
    00-010519

Text and Illustrations © 1999 by Mick Manning and Brita Granström
Published in 2001 by Albert Whitman & Company,
6340 Oakton Street, Morton Grove, Illinois 60053-2723.
Published simultaneously in Canada
by General Publishing, Limited, Toronto.
Printed in Singapore.
10 9 8 7 6 5 4 3 2 1